The Monster Story-Teller

...as an ordinary flower-patterned saucer. But today it had grown wings.

"Of course!" said Natalie. "It's a flying saucer!"

She went to have a closer look.

There was a little creature standing in the saucer.

Was it an ant?

"A flying ant!" Natalie giggled.

It wasn't an ant.

It was a very, very, very tiny monster.

D0480684

Also available by Jacqueline Wilson

Published in Corgi Pups, for beginner readers:
THE DINOSAUR'S PACKED LUNCH
THE MONSTER STORY-TELLER

Published in Young Corgi, for newly confident readers:
LIZZIE ZIPMOUTH
SLEEPOVERS

Available from Doubleday/Corgi Yearling Books:
BAD GIRLS
THE BED & BREAKFAST STAR
BEST FRIENDS
BURIED ALIVE!
CANDYFLOSS
THE CAT MUMMY
CLEAN BREAK
CLIFFHANGER
THE DARE GAME
THE DIAMOND GIRLS
DOUBLE ACT
DOUBLE ACT (PLAY EDITION)
GLUBBSLYME
THE ILLUSTRATED MUM
JACKY DAYDREAM
THE LOTTIE PROJECT
MIDNIGHT
THE MUM-MINDER
SECRETS
STARRING TRACY BEAKER
THE STORY OF TRACY BEAKER
THE SUITCASE KID
VICKY ANGEL
THE WORRY WEBSITE

Join the official Jacqueline Wilson fan club at
www.jacquelinewilson.co.uk

The Monster Story-Teller

The Monster Story-Teller

Jacqueline Wilson

Illustrated by Nick Sharratt

CORGI PUPS

THE MONSTER STORY-TELLER
A CORGI PUPS BOOK 978 0 552 55787 0

First published in Great Britain by Doubleday,
an imprint of Random House Children's Publishers UK
A Random House Group Company

Doubleday edition published 1997
First Corgi Pups edition published 1997
This Corgi Pups edition published 2008

13

Text copyright © Jacqueline Wilson, 1997
Illustrations copyright © Nick Sharratt, 1997

The right of Jacqueline Wilson to be identified as the author of this work has been asserted
in accordance with the Copyright, Designs and Patents Act 1988.

All rights reserved. No part of this publication may be reproduced, stored in a retrieval system,
or transmitted in any form or by any means, electronic, mechanical, photocopying,
recording or otherwise, without the prior permission of the publishers.

Set in 19/23 Bembo Infant

Young Corgi Books are published by Random House Children's Publishers UK,
61–63 Uxbridge Road, London W5 5SA

www.**randomhousechildrens**.co.uk
www.randomhouse.co.uk

Addresses for companies within The Random House Group Limited can be found at:
www.randomhouse.co.uk/offices.htm

THE RANDOM HOUSE GROUP Limited Reg. No. 954009

A CIP catalogue record for this book is available from the British Library.

The Random House Group Limited supports The Forest Stewardship
Council® (FSC®), the leading international forest-certification organisation.
Our books carrying the FSC label are printed on FSC®-certified paper.
FSC is the only forest-certification scheme supported by the leading
environmental organisations, including Greenpeace. Our
paper procurement policy can be found at
www.randomhouse.co.uk/environment

MIX
Paper from
responsible sources
FSC® C016897

Printed and bound in Great Britain by Clays Ltd, St Ives plc

For Sean William MacLahlan

DUDLEY PUBLIC LIBRARIES	
000000984621	
£5.99	JF
01-Oct-2015	PETERS
JFP	

CONTENTS

Series Reading Consultant: Prue Goodwin
Reading and Language Information Centre,
University of Reading

Chapter One

Natalie was fed up.

The class were doing a project on flying.

She had made a big bird but his wings went wonky. He wouldn't fly.

Natalie talked to her friends.

"What did you do on Saturday?" Natalie asked.

"I went swimming," said Clare.

"I went to McDonald's," said Zoe.

"I went to the football match," said Lee.

"I went shopping with my nan," said Clive. "She gave me five pounds. And she bought me chocolates. Yum yum."

"Do you want to hear what I did on Saturday?" said Natalie. "First I went swimming and there were real dolphins in the pool and they gave me a ride. Then I went to McDonald's and I had twenty Big Macs and twenty strawberry milk shakes. And then

I went to this football match and I was the mascot and I scored a goal and everyone cheered. And then I went shopping with my nan and she gave me fifty pounds and lots and lots and lots of chocolates."

"How many chocolates?" said Clive.

"Natalie's telling stories, silly," said Lee.

"Settle down, children!" said Mr Hunter. "Natalie, get on with your work and stop telling stories. It's not story-time until this afternoon – when we're going to have a special treat."

"I want a special treat now,"
Natalie muttered. "This is boring,
boring, boring."

She sighed.

She stretched.

She looked up at the window.
She looked at the plant in the pot
on the window sill.

And the plant in the pot moved.

Natalie blinked.

The plant in the pot moved again. Upwards!

Was the plant in the pot flying? Then Natalie saw!

The plant in the pot wasn't flying.

It was the saucer.

It was an ordinary flower-patterned saucer. But today it had grown wings.

"Of course!" said Natalie. "It's
a flying saucer!"

She went to have a closer look.

There was a little creature
standing in the saucer.

Was it an ant?

"A flying ant!" Natalie giggled.

It wasn't an ant.

It was a very, very, very tiny
monster.

It had wild hair and pointy
teeth and sharp claws and a long
tail.

But it didn't look fierce. It
looked friendly.

"Hello!" said Natalie.

"Hello!" said the tiny monster.

"Can you speak up a bit?" said Natalie. "I can't hear you properly."

"I'm shouting!" said the tiny monster. "Can you speak down a bit? You're hurting my ears."

"Is it your flying saucer?" Natalie whispered, so softly her lips scarcely moved.

The tiny monster nodded proudly.

"Want to see me do twirlie-whirlies?" he said.

"You bet!" said Natalie.

The tiny monster tapped his teeny foot.

The saucer flapped its little wings and whizzed round and round in the air. The plant's leaves waved wildly.

The tiny monster waved too as he circled Natalie's head, round and round until she got dizzy.

The plant wobbled and wobbled until...

...it tipped right off the saucer and crashed onto the classroom floor!

"Oh help!" said the tiny monster.

"Oh help!" said Natalie. "What's Mr Hunter going to say?"

Chapter Two

Mr Hunter said plenty.
"You naughty girl, Natalie!

What were you doing over by the window? Did you knock that plant over on purpose?"

"No! It wasn't me," said Natalie.

"It was me!" said the tiny monster, flying his saucer behind Natalie.

"Look at the mess on the floor! Go and fetch a dustpan and brush from the store cupboard, Natalie," said Mr Hunter. "And take that silly smile off your face. It isn't funny."

Natalie couldn't help smiling. The tiny monster was tickling the back of her neck with his weeny claws.

Natalie hurried out of the classroom.

The flying saucer went with her, whirling round her head.

"Where are you going?" shouted the tiny monster.

"To fetch the dustpan and brush," said Natalie.

"Boring, boring, boring," said the tiny monster. "Come flying with me instead. Jump up on my saucer."

"I can't," said Natalie. "I'm much too big. I'd smash the saucer. And squash you."

"I can make you small," said the tiny monster. "Hold my hand."

Natalie held out her great big hand. The tiny monster held out his weeny little paw.

Then Natalie started shrinking!

She felt as if she were being rubbed with very powerful magic soap.

She got smaller and smaller and smaller until she was exactly the same size as the tiny monster. Only he didn't look tiny now.

The monster's hair was very wild.

His teeth were very pointy.

His claws were very sharp.

His tail was very long.

But he still didn't look fierce.

He looked friendly.

"Let's fly," said the monster. "Shall we go fast?"

"You bet!" said Natalie.

The monster tapped his paw and the wings flapped very fast indeed. The flying saucer whizzed way down the school corridor.

"Aaaaah!" said Natalie.

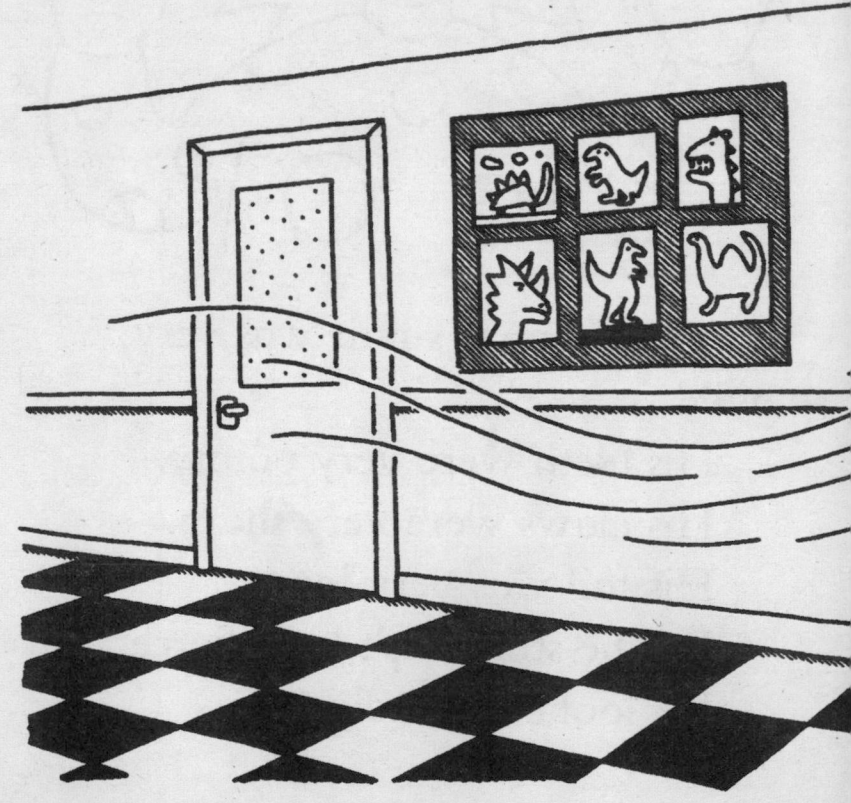

"This is easy-peasy slowcoach stuff," said the monster, showing off like mad. "Let's go outside."

Natalie nodded.

She didn't have any breath left for talking.

They flew very fast across the
playground.

"Wheeeeee!" said Natalie.
"This is wonderful! Can we go
right over the rooftops?"

"You bet!" said the monster.

They did twirlie-whirlies round
the chimney-pots.

"Now let's do swoopie-
doopies," said the monster.

They swooped right down to
the park.

The duck pond looked like a
puddle from high in the sky, but
when they got nearer and
nearer...

...the ducks started to get bigger and bigger.

"Quick! Fly up or they'll get us!" said Natalie.

"Chicken," teased the monster.

"No – duck!" said Natalie.

They swooped up just in time, leaving the ducks quacking foolishly.

"I live near the park," said
Natalie. "There's my house.
Look, there's my mum and my
little brothers!"

"Hey, do you want to see my
mum and my little brothers?" said
the monster.

"You bet!" said Natalie.

"OK. Monster Planet, here we come!"

Chapter Three

The flying saucer's wings grew immensely.

They flapped faster and faster and faster.

The flying saucer shot straight into the sky. It flew higher than the tallest buildings in the whole world...

...higher than the world itself, away to a different planet altogether.

Monster Planet.

"There it is!" shouted the monster.

"It's little!" said Natalie.

"So are we," said the monster.

"I can see water," said Natalie.

"It's our seaside," said the monster.

"I can see lots of little monster people!" said Natalie.

They had wild hair and pointy teeth and sharp claws and long tails. But they didn't look fierce. They looked friendly.

"Shall we go for a sail?" said the monster.

"You bet!" said Natalie. "Hey, do you have dolphins?"

"Watch!" said the monster, and he whistled.

Six special monster dolphins
leapt out of the water and
whistled back.

The smiliest special monster
dolphin gave Natalie a ride.

"That was wonderful," said
Natalie. "But I'm all wet now."

"We have special drying dragons on the beach," said the monster, parking the flying saucer.

"Do you want the warm dragon, the hot dragon, or the special sauna dragon?" said the monster.

"Just the warm one, please,"
said Natalie.

She was wonderfully warm in
seconds.

The monster had the special
sauna treatment and was so red-
hot he fried an egg on himself
and ate it!

"Do you want an egg too, Natalie?" said the monster.

"Maybe not an egg," said Natalie. "But I am starving."

"Do you want to go to McMonsters?" said the monster.

"You bet!" said Natalie.

Natalie ate a McMonster burger. And another and another and another.

Whenever she got thirsty she went to the pretty pink fountain. It was strawberry monster milk shake!

"I think I'm full up now," said
Natalie.

"Let's go and look round the
shops," said the monster.

"I haven't got any money,"
said Natalie.

"No problem," said the
monster. "Monster money grows
on trees, look. Just help yourself!"

So Natalie and the monster
picked a pocketful of monster
money and went to the monster
shopping centre.

There was a monster pet shop with monster dogs and monster cats and monster rabbits and monster hamsters and monster mice.

Natalie liked the monster birds best. She bought them all so she could let them out of their cages.

The monster birds flapped their wings and flew far away.

"Let's go in the sports shop," said the monster.

"Yes! I'll buy that football," said Natalie.

"Who do you support?" said the monster. "I like the Monster Marvels."

"Me too," said Natalie.

"Do you want to go to the match?" said the monster.

"You bet!" said Natalie.

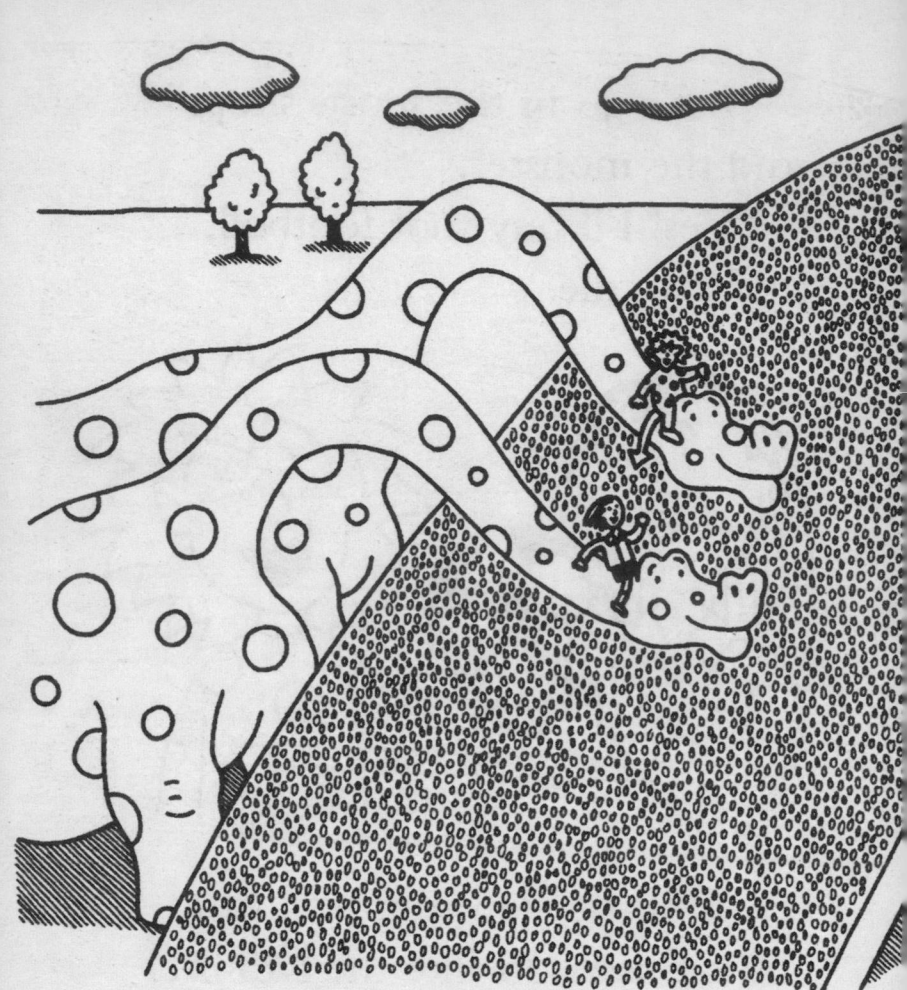

The monster football stadium
was packed out.

Natalie and the monster got
specially shown to their seats.

"Up the Monster Marvels!"
yelled Natalie.

They all waved to her when
they ran onto the pitch.

"Come and kick off for us,
Natalie," they shouted.

Natalie scored a stupendous goal.

"Hurray for Natalie!" shouted all the monsters, while she leapt in the air.

The monster took Natalie to meet his monster nan after the match.

Monster Nan made a great fuss of them both. She gave them hot chocolate to drink and cold chocolate ice-cream to eat – and lots and lots and lots of chocolate bars.

"Don't tell your mum or she'll fuss about your teeth," said Monster Nan.

"I want to see your mum and your little brothers," said Natalie.

"Right," said the monster. "Hop back on the flying saucer."

They flew over the monster's house.

"There they are! That's my monster mum. And my little monster brothers."

"My brothers are little monsters too!" said Natalie.

"Why aren't you at school, you bad little monster?" shouted his monster mum.

"Uh oh. School!" said the monster.

"Off you go!" said Monster Mum.

They flew to Monster School.
The monster teacher had wild
hair and pointy teeth and sharp
claws and a long tail.

He looked very fierce.

He didn't look friendly.

"Where on earth have you
been? And who is this strange
girl?" said the monster teacher.

"She's my friend Natalie from
another planet. We've whizzed
back here from Earth," said the
monster.

"You're telling stories again!" said the monster teacher. "You're in big trouble, little monster."

"Oh help!" said the monster. "Let's go, Natalie!"

They jumped back on the saucer.

"Planet Earth, ever so quickly, please!" said the monster.

The saucer flew down and down and down, all the way back to Earth...

...right above Natalie's school.

"I don't think I want to go back," said Natalie. "I think I might be in big trouble too. I'd sooner stay with you and have MONSTER FUN."

Chapter Four

"I don't want to say goodbye!"
said Natalie.

"Don't worry. I'll come back,"
said the monster.

"Promise?" said Natalie.

"You bet!" said the monster.

Natalie got ready to jump off
the saucer. Then she saw a
HUGE monster.

"Aaaaah!" said Natalie.

"Miaow," said the huge monster.

"It's the school cat!" said Natalie. "But it's much bigger than me now."

"Shake my hand, silly," said the monster. "Then you'll grow big again."

Natalie clasped the monster's paw and immediately started growing again.

"Get off my saucer before I get squashed!" said the tiny monster.

Natalie jumped to the ground as she grew to her proper size.

She waved goodbye, stroked the cat, grabbed the dustpan and brush, and ran back to her classroom.

"Natalie!" shouted Mr Hunter. "Where on earth have you been?"

"I haven't been anywhere on Earth, Mr Hunter. Wait till I tell you," said Natalie.

She told everyone her story about Monster Planet. Everyone loved Natalie's story. Everyone but Mr Hunter.

"You're telling stories again, Natalie!"

Guess what. Natalie was in big trouble.

Natalie cheered up that afternoon. A special visitor came to the school. A story-teller.

She told the children stories about mice and clowns and princes and elephants and gingerbread men.

"And now I'll tell you my favourite story," said the story-teller. "It's all about monsters!"

"Once upon a time there was this very, very, very tiny monster with wild hair and pointy teeth and sharp claws and a long tail. This tiny monster had his very own flying saucer," said the story-teller.

"That's Natalie's story!" said all the children. "Natalie's told us that story already, Miss."

"Come out here, Natalie. So you like telling stories?" said the story-teller.

"You bet!" said Natalie.

"Maybe you'll be a story-teller like me when you grow up."

"Do you want to tell the Monster Story, Natalie?" said the story-teller.

"Well, it is my story," said Natalie.

"It's my story too," said a teeny tiny voice.

So they all told the Monster Story together.

THE END

ABOUT THE AUTHOR

JACQUELINE WILSON is one of Britain's most outstanding writers for young readers. She is the most borrowed author from British libraries and has sold over 25 million books in this country. As a child, she always wanted to be a writer and wrote her first 'novel' when she was nine, filling countless exercise books as she grew up. She started work at a publishing company and then went on to work as a journalist on *Jackie* magazine (which was named after her) before turning to writing fiction full-time.

Jacqueline has been honoured with many of the UK's top awards for children's books, including the Guardian Children's Fiction Award, the Smarties Prize, the Red House Book Award and the Children's Book of the Year. She was awarded an OBE in 2002 and was the Children's Laureate for 2005-2007.

ABOUT THE ILLUSTRATOR

NICK SHARRATT knew from an early age that
he wanted to use his drawing skills as his career,
so he went to Manchester Polytechnic to do an
Art Foundation course. He followed this up with
a BA (Hons) in Graphic Design at St. Martin's
School of Art in London from 1981–1984.

Since graduating, Nick has been working full-time
as an illustrator for children's books, publishers and
a wide range of magazines. His brilliant illustrations
have brought to life many books, most notably
the titles by Jacqueline Wilson.

Nick also writes books as well as illustrating them.

THE DINOSAUR'S PACKED LUNCH
Jacqueline Wilson

"A hand reached out and patted Dinah on
the shoulder. A huge scaly hand with
a spiked thumb . . ."

On a school trip to see the dinosaurs in the
museum, everyone in the class has a packed lunch.
Everyone, that is, except for Dinah. Until a
friendly iguanodon decides to help . . .

Soon Dinah has a very special packed lunch -
and a huge surprise to come!

ISBN: 978 0 552 55782 5

LIZZIE ZIPMOUTH
Jacqueline Wilson

"Why don't you ever say anything, Lizzie?"
said Rory. "It's like you've got a zip
across your mouth."

Lizzie refuses to speak.

She doesn't want to talk to Rory or Jake, her new
stepbrothers, or Sam, their dad, or even her mum.
She's totally fed up at having to join a new family
and nothing can coax her into speaking to them.
Not football, not pizza, not a new bedroom.
That is, until she meets a member of the new
family who is even more stubborn than her -
and has had a lot more practice!

ISBN: 978 0 552 55784 9

SLEEPOVERS
Jacqueline Wilson

**Sleepover parties are the greatest!
Everybody's having one . . .**

All of Daisy's friends in the Alphabet Club – Amy,
Bella, Chloe and Emily, have had sleepovers for their
birthdays. Daisy has a dilemma. She'd love to have a
sleepover too, but then she'd have to let her
friends meet her sister...

A funny and moving story for younger readers
from the award-winning author of *Lizzie Zipmouth*
and *Double Act*.

ISBN: 978 0 552 55783 2

THE WORRY WEBSITE
Jacqueline Wilson

Type in your worry . . .

Is anything bothering you? Problems in class or
at home? Don't know where to turn for help?
Log on to the Worry Website! Type in your worry
and wait for the good advice to flow in.

At least that's the plan when Mr Speed sets up his
super-cool new Worry Website for the class. Holly,
Greg, Natasha and the rest feel that they've got
shedloads of worries but, as they find out,
sometimes the best advice comes from the most
unexpected place.

A fabulous collection of linked short stories from the
bestselling, award-winning Jacqueline Wilson.
Also includes a prize-winning story by a
12-year-old writer!

ISBN: 978 0 440 86826 2

THE MUM-MINDER
Jacqueline Wilson

"I'm Sadie and I'm nearly nine. Mum's a
childminder, but she doesn't have to mind me.
I can mind myself, easy-peasy. Lucky for Mum,
because now she's got the flu, so I've got to
mind her - and help with all the babies!"

A hilarious, entertaining and lively account,
told throughout in Sadie's own words, of one
chaotic week in the life of a young girl whose
mother is a childminder.

ISBN: 978 0 440 86825 5